THE SEX OF THE ANGELS,
THE SAINTS IN THEIR HEAVEN

THE GERMAN LIST

THE SEX
OF THE
ANGELS,
THE SAINTS
IN THEIR
HEAVEN
A Breviary

Raoul Schrott

Illustrated by
Arnold Mario Dall'O

TRANSLATED BY KAREN LEEDER

Seagull
BOOKS

CALCUTTA LONDON NEW YORK

This publication was supported by a grant from the Austrian Federal
Ministry for Education, Arts and Culture, and the Goethe-Institut India.

Seagull Books, 2018

Originally published in German as *Das Geschlecht der Engel,
der Himmel der Heiligen*

© Carl Hanser Verlag, Munich, 2001

First published in English translation by Seagull Books, 2018

English translation © Karen Leeder, 2018

ISBN 978 0 8574 2 555 3

British Library Cataloguing-in-Publication Data
A catalogue record for this book is available
from the British Library.

Typeset and designed by Sunandini Banerjee, Seagull Books
Printed and bound by Hyam Enterprises, Calcutta, India

Me ne stavo qui con gli occhiali al soffitto
a innamorarmi dei colori delle cose
ma desiderare non basta
da così lontano non basta
Ora ho un contratto con gli angeli
e ti ritrovo di sicuro vita
in qualche mese d'agosto accecante
o in un tempo meno illuso che vuoi tu
Perché la vita non va così
è la disciplina della terra

Ivano Fossati

Dionysius the
Areopagite, Syrian
scholar of the fifth
century, often identi-
fied in the Middle
Ages with Saint
Dionysius of Paris;
just as things become
ever darker the
further they are
removed from
the sun of God, he
wrote in the *Celestial
Hierarchy,* so the nine
choirs of his angels
are able to reflect His
light less and less
from order to order.

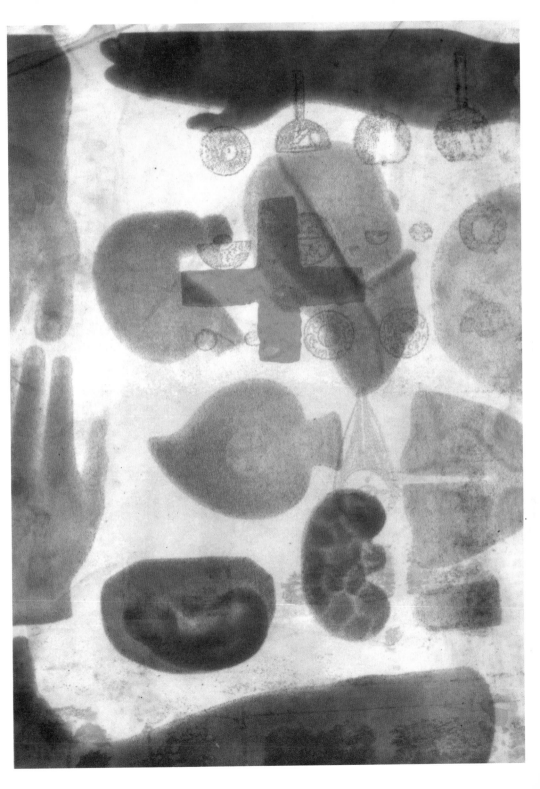

I

Dionysius the Areopagite was, I believe, the first to order the eternal night of the universe with angels. At the turn of the fifth century, this Syrian monk shaped the whirring throng of demigods and daemons into the image of a unified world by having them keep the stars in motion. To the outermost sphere, the dwelling reserved for God, the *primum mobile* of the fixed stars, he assigned the Cherubim and Seraphim; and to each of the planets circling within he designated a choir of angels: seven

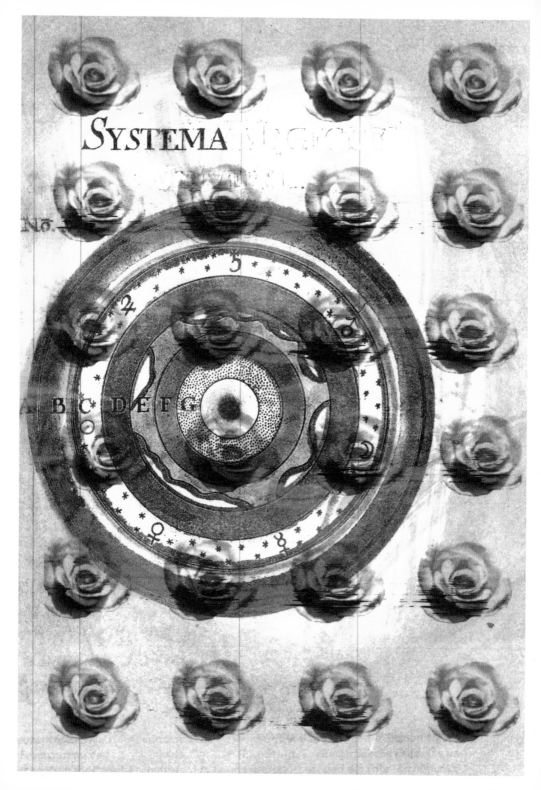

orders, from the Thrones of Saturn to the Virtues of Venus; the Archangels of Mercury to the Angels of the moon. For Earth he chose only a single one, which he placed in the lower left arc of my ribs where I can feel it now, hard as a little planet. I carry it with me (even now in the train it keeps to its orbit) and sometimes I can see it before me: its mouth, black brows and a storm of red hair over its freckles, an incarnation of St Elmo's fire. Its conception was immaculate (it knows nothing of it), a half-puzzled surprise in the dog days of summer: August in a half-empty city. Its annunciation fell on a Tuesday and since that day the four cardinal points have receded as never before, revealing the translucent vault of the heavens; one can see as far as the furthest spheres and the world has become too vast to hold.

Rosa of Lima wore a crown of thorns made of iron hidden beneath a garland of roses in her shining red hair. As a child, her face had been seen transforming into a mystic rose; when she was sanctified, the heavens raged and a rain of roses fell.

Nothing but a trick, I'm sure. The work of fallen angels— or at least the ones who've stumbled across me here. I could have hired a few stragglers from the lowest orders in secret, poor devils, out-of-work actors, just waiting for a sign from me to ambush you and spirit you away, had it not been for that *non licet* gate, to which only the chosen have the key. As it was, a few hasty words escaped my lips before I knew it, and there was nothing for it but to bow and scrape and take my leave. More fool me; but, for all that, not fool enough to imagine anything could come of it. I tried to keep countenance at least.

Whichever way it is: when one is being prompted by one of the Dominions of Jupiter or the Principalities of Mars, it's only too easy to fall out of character. You of course were perfect, your mask flawless. But let me assure you: should the planets ever be realigned in this conjunction, I would appear as impartial as that saint who tried to rebuke the storm. Or an angel—just a little bit berserk. I only wish I could see you now curled up in your chair, that sceptical look on your face, and how you were simply the most wonderful thing anyone could imagine. Would it embarrass you terribly if I told you that you're beautiful? Hardly, I suppose.

Addendum for the Night

is Lake Zurich, the half-timbered buildings, Iona and Stäffa, both towns obviously founded by wandering Scottish monks. And St Gallen, founded by the Irish a bit further up in the North. The lake quiet. A three-quarter moon, yellow and low. Thinking of you I catch my breath. And it's good. The *primum mobile* of the night.

II

The angels originally had their wings attached to their feet; that white instep so covered with freckles that . . . (that much I knew already; but how did you bruise your right big toe?). This because they had to embody Hermes, the god of all messengers, but more likely also to accentuate their swiftness, the way they circle in perfect, eternal orbits the imperfect and ever-changing Earth. They were thought of as personifications of the stars and of the ubiquitous influence of the constellations on animals, plants and man; as allegories of the Fates, in a syncretism of Christianity and the then-dominant science of astrology. Ah, the exact sciences.

This whole time I've been thinking about angels in terms of cause and effect, in order to make sense of what has happened to me. But I can't put it down to their pirouettes alone—nor these flushed cheeks, the dry throat. Effects everywhere, but nothing to suggest any kind of cause. There was nothing inevitable or unforeseen, only you, in majuscule, looking up to the gallery and saying hello. I've been searching for the right word, to give it a name, but only one etymology has occurred to me, one that leads back to the angels: infatuation, *fatum*, *fata* and *fatuus*: fate, fay and fool. And me, who is a fool in the absence of fates and faeries that foretell his fate; in the absence of you.

And now I hear your voice in my ear like the breath between two sentences, you stand before me in your white blouse, sleeves rolled up, narrow black trousers, a few untidy strands of hair tumbling down, the surprised, almost mischievous look, and your head suddenly turned to me, a shock of dark red hair. I wish you had come back; even if we had missed each other, it would be nothing compared to how I miss you now. But why? There was nothing, not even a glance or a word that might have emboldened me in my circumlocutions then or now. You were flawless, not a gesture out of place.

The exact sciences. What there is nowadays of angels can be found under www.pfrr.alaska.edu/pfrr-/aurora. There is still debate as to whether one can hear the Northern Lights. Or whether parhelia make a sound; these are sundogs, the mock suns

Saint Conrad the hermit: he renounced his passion for the hunt, after he burnt down a local forest while hunting and went into the mountains, where the birds sang for him. He separated from his wife Euphrosyne when Fate stood before him in the form of a red-headed angel.

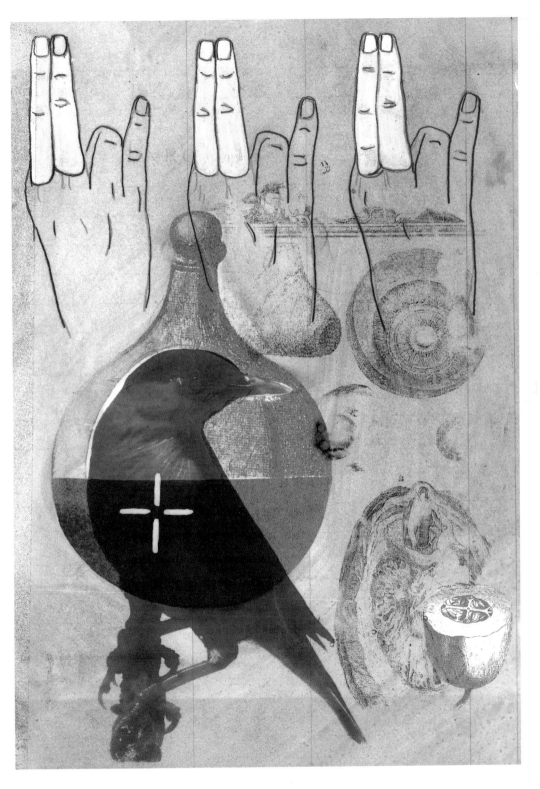

formed by the refraction of ice crystals in the air when the sun is close to the horizon, bright shining points created to left and right of it. I, for one, run round in circles, panting and wagging my tail. I can hardly contain myself (in a cultivated fashion, I mean). I'm restless, can't tear my thoughts from you, can't sleep—along with the rest of the catalogue of sorry symptoms.

Poets and lovers are always afflicted by some kind of infatuation, from which they can only be cured by absence. So said Dr Samuel Johnson, even if only with an eye to his encyclopaedia, I'm sure. Judging by that I am safe from all such delusions: (a) because (to take up the challenge of other poets immortalizing you) I don't have even a halfway decent poem to set before you. Just the incredible sheer blue that day that kept sliding from view, the sky that receded further and further and you coming closer and closer, until there you were: suddenly standing before me at breakfast that morning in the garden, your hair still wet.

And coming back to Johnson: (b) absence has made everything worse. So, what is to be done? The only logical conclusion is that I must see you again. I promise I'll refrain from any ardour under your balcony and desist from serving up stories about angels. My every gesture would make perfect sense. I would meet you in Lisbon, Livorno or London, in alphabetical or chronological order, disguised as Arsène Lupin, with a false beard, a top hat, glasses on my nose and my hair parted the wrong way, for all I care. It goes without saying that I insist on nothing; it behoves one ill when one sets out to entertain an angel.

Rosalia of Palermo; her bones were only discovered after five hundred years in a cave on Mount Pellegrino. She lay as if in a kind of rapture, eyes half-closed, head resting carelessly on her right hand, as if in conversation with an angel who seemed to be fanning her to cool her.

III

The Fates, goddesses of fate, once more: Clotho, Lachesis and Atropos, that turn the world on its axis, moving the seven celestial spheres of the cosmos like so many spindles inside one another; weaving a thread that is spun on Clotho's spindle, measured with Lachesis' rod, to be snipped with Atropos' shears. The daughters of necessity. Present, past and future in their platonic order. And on each of the seven spheres in the boundless space between the angels' circular spandrels: the sirens turning and turning, singing: a single chord. That's how the angels came into being, that's how they began, and those were the original sounds of their language. What language do the angels speak, you ask? English of course, Anglo-Saxon. But Anglo- and angel? Or as they're actually called, *Angles* and *angels*?

Only after thousands of years did their common origin manifest itself. For nothing appeared to link their Greek roots: angel was *aggelos*, the mounted messenger; angle stems from *agkulos*, bent, curved, like a river, an anchor, an arm. Only in Latin did they begin to get closer, *angelus* and *angulus*, the latter not appearing as a word until the Middle Ages and then chiefly in the West. They were only depicted with wings from the fifth century onwards. But what brought angle and angel into such proximity? Perhaps just a mispronunciation. Or possibly the fact that angle was originally understood as an ankle: the joint where instep and shin come to meet, the heel where the angels sprouted their wings.

Granted, these etymologies might seem a little farfetched (like all academic derivations) if they did not allow me to come back to you once more: shoes off, legs stretched out towards the fire, the

Phocas, patron of gardeners and mariners; he lived on the banks of a river at the Black Sea and took in travellers, letting them stay at his house without charge. Accused by a resentful neighbour, he offered hospitality to the soldiers on horseback that came to arrest him, thereby digging his own grave.

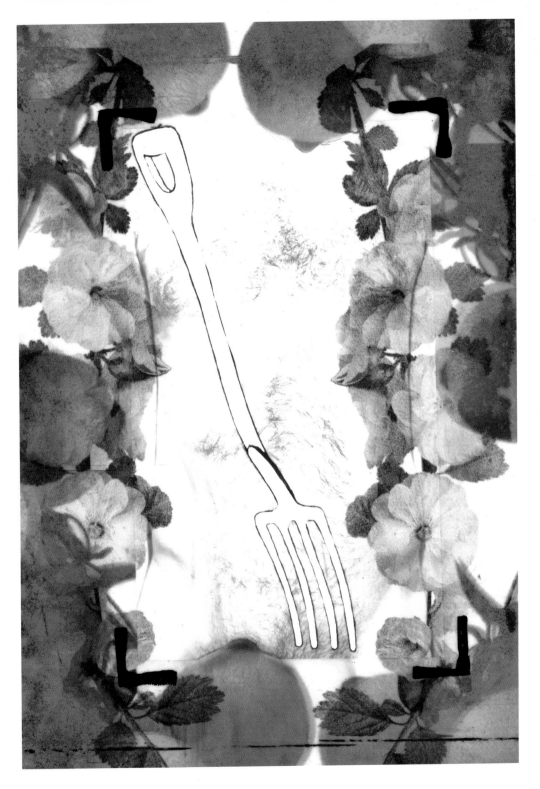

olive green of your suit, the white of your ankle (contrary to what you must be thinking by now, I am not a foot-fetishist; it was the only place my gaze could stray secretly—and hopefully without being noticed). The one naked thing. The closest I got to you. The first chapter of my Angelography. An allegory like all allegories: speaking about that which cannot be known.

So, what do I know of you? I can only recall with any certainty the way you moved. Your demeanour, your composure, your poise; at the same time something decisive, determined, in it—the way you rested your weight on the inside of your knees and your heels as if you were standing on stage reading. Laughter didn't come that easily to you (I'm not so sure about that now). The way you spoke about charlatans—and me taking it as a sign that I must be making a little headway at least. The way you picked up the thread from the day before. In spite of everything, that naturalness about you: the tone of your voice, the way it rested on every word, not a single glance that strayed over to me; how I wondered, how I was wounded, by that. Something severe too: *Ring the alarum bell!—Blow, wind! Come, wrack! At least we'll die with harness on our back.*

I exaggerate, I know, but only to fill in the gaps. Idealizations being in the end what they are: they rest on ideas. Even taking all that into account, there's not much left to help me piece you together. But enough all the same. A likeness. And for that reason I wish there were something I could give you as a gift, not something that has to do with words, not something obvious but self-evident nonetheless. It will come to me.

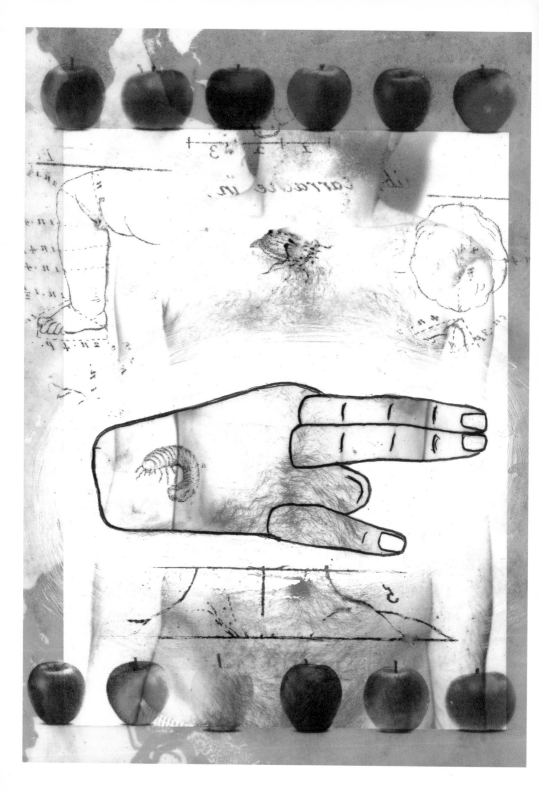

Addendum for the Night

The snow is melting, the river 20 feet deep, full of tree
trunks. The hot fall winds; the mountains foregrounded,
as if coloured by hand. The birches green as birch. Letters,
so I have you somewhere between my fingers and the
page.

Malachy O'Morgair,
Archbishop of
Armagh, who
founded the first
Cistercian monastery
in Ireland. According
to Bernard of Clair-
vaux, he possessed
second sight and
could heal kings by
presenting them
with an apple; he
perished in a flood
in the South of
France. His bones
were mixed with
those of Saint
Bernard during the
French Revolution.

19

IV

Prophesy spoke though fire, water, earth and air, the oak tree there and its branches in the wind, the tongues of the Hamadryads, the surf and spray of the Nereids and nymphs, Sibyls, the Muses, the grace of the Charites and the world as it splinters into different voices, numberless voices, between what they say and what they are. Until Dionysius the Areopagite united the four elements again and transformed them into a fifth, the quintessence of the highest heaven: the Empyream. Made only of fire and air and its angels of pure light. They were what could be seen, *idein*: the idea; and calling to them, *kalein*, brought about beauty: *kalos*. And yet I've no idea what his angels say. (I'm no mystic.) Perhaps the idea that your beauty implies something beyond the merely human, in the sense of a beauty that shares all the qualities of fire, earth, water and air: a figure, a form, which is a memory of a reality otherwise indifferent and inaccessible.

I still recall making my farewells in the courtyard and kissing your cheek twice (a few days ago I read in the paper that the English hate to be kissed on the cheek, women even more so than men). I'd imagined it as hard and firm, but found it soft. That is practically the only moment of eroticism that I can recall (and describe). Finding your invitation slipped under the oak door, and still knowing nothing, not then, at least. Then as I sat next to you in the great hall, I heard you more than saw you beside me; I listened to you; wings folding shut. Do I bore you with all these sophistries and sentimentalities? It is only because the post takes so damned long, because I don't know whether you will ever respond, nor how; because I must eke out the little that I have to create a picture of you: little stones for a mosaic. The angels help me lay it out.

And anyway, apart from that, I know next to nothing about you. And I'm still wracking my brains as to why, with such distance between us, then as now, I feel so close to you. Of course I can think of reasons that make everything appear less inevitable and unforeseen, than I am making out here. Nevertheless. At least in the meantime I've found the right word for it, for now at least. Of the English terms *desire*, *lust*, *yearning* and *longing*, it is the last one that's right: the birthmark of an angel is also called a *longing mark*. But of the German equivalents—*Begehren*, *Sehnsucht*, *Verlangen*, *Begier* and *Begierde*—the first is mine.

There's no escaping such angels. How much happier I would be telling you about Pan, about satyrs, Silenus and fauns, gnomes and gargoyles, or old Irish leprechauns, cluricaunes, lurikeen and Korrigans, all the unholy Elven of Tara: *tara, tara tara, full East and by South; we sail with thunder in our mouth, we bustle along, through the heavenly throng*. I only wish I had enough English in me to steer this course and throw the OED overboard. To see you swimming away before the storm in that favourite painting of yours, as the saints puff out their cheeks. If that's really you in the bottom left-hand corner, where are you heading in a Force Eight gale? In any case, it won't be me reefing the sails even if they should tear. You, by contrast, must be fire and earth.

Adelhaide, Empress of the Holy Roman Empire, who withdrew to an abbey. Depicted with a small ship in her hand, in which she fled her imprisonment; a fisherman brought her secretly across Lake Garda during a storm, though he himself perished.

V

The Angels to the Areopagite were *noes*: creations of thought. The singular, *nous*, denoted a self-ruled 'being unto itself'—that which keeps the cosmic spheres in motion, the *spiritus mundi*. For all that can be imagined also exists. And in order to give thoughts a body and with it a world, he called them angels and transported them to paradise. You can't get there with the usual pathos; instead, you must turn to Pothos, god of yearning. Though without Eros' companion Peitho, goddess of persuasion, there is no hope of success, since *erotaien* means to question

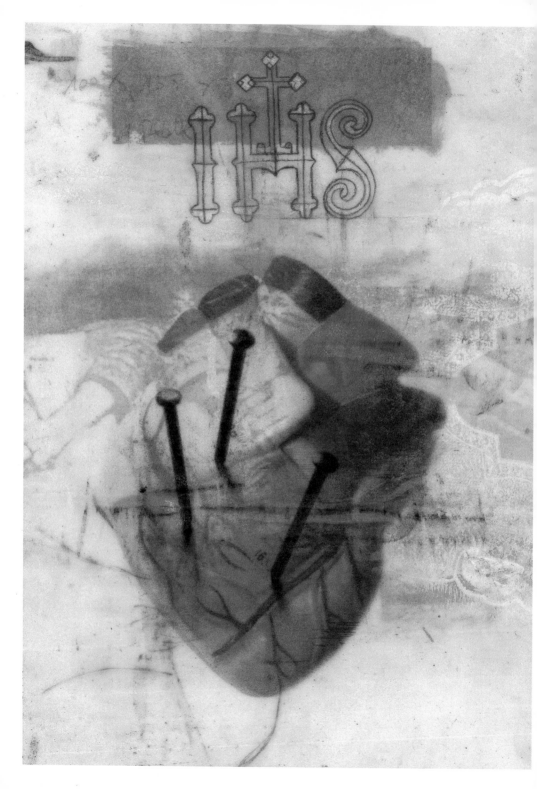

(*erotesis* the figure of speech that implies the opposite of what is asked).

So: let me now be bold, eloquent and impertinent, let me be the one who knows it all. Dionysius' angels are a Roman battalion that stands under arms, ready for battle. Yet these hierarchies also harbour their opposite numbers, their counterparts; the choruses of the Erotes: and that's where we derive our Cupids and Amores, with their bow and their quiver.

I am shooting arrows into the night; I'm shooting nothing but arrows into the night. There are near-Earth asteroids, called the Amors, and sometimes they pass close to the moon. It will rise in the next ten minutes, here against the mountain; in its halo you can already see the silhouette of the firs along the ridge. And then I will make the sky anew for you (like Douglas Adams that time, drunk as a skunk in the grass at the camp site in Innsbruck, beer can balanced on his nose, looking up at the stars and getting the inspiration for the *Hitchhikers' Guide to the Galaxy*). The moon, its rim now, aluminium; the bottom of the can. Perhaps it will soon go 'plop' and 'tssssssssssss'. . . It rolls out of the branches, the foehn wind still gusting. Now it comes to rest, perfectly balanced (let the post

Ignatius of Loyola, the army chief of the King of Navarre, who lived a life of wanton gambling and brawling until he was finally vanquished by the sins of the flesh and a cannonball. Appointed himself Superior General of the Compañia de Jesu, and ordained spiritual exercises thirty times a day to keep all amorous adventures at bay.

bring a letter from you at last, or this will all get as long-winded as a Teutonic treatise on the nature of serifs and Seraphim—and me all at sea on account of all these angels).

Well, then, what shall we concoct for ourselves now? Something like: the moon was once an old sun; when it was no use any more for the day, it was moved to the night. But night is not simply night. What you see are gullies and gorges, the high plains and valleys of a dark country. The stars are the torches of the Amores held up there by a storm (of course these are windproof storm torches, the very the latest American design, so they don't go out). But when the wind drops they descend towards us, the Amores: decked out in all their armour, lances, swords and chains, and only the cupids have forgotten to pull their clothes on again. They swoop down on us like frigate birds or albatrosses. Have you ever seen them landing on the sea? They can only take off from the crest of a wave if there's enough wind.

It's an antipodean country, as I said, dark foothills and a black ocean. Flowers grow on the headlands, but because there is so little soil, they cannot take hold and are blown

clean away: these are the Leonid showers (I've enclosed a
specimen with this letter, it's what we down here call
Himmelschlüssel, 'heaven's key', but to you it is merely a
cowslip). And the ocean is criss-crossed by ships (manned
by whom and belonging to whom, I've no idea), that
use their sail as a keel and their keel as a sail. That they
exist is proved by Germaine de Tilbury's description of
an anchor that fell onto English soil at three in the afternoon, close to Guildford, with the chain still dangling
through the clouds. And as for this naked red-haired
woman, suddenly swimming up in the right-hand corner,
now I know where she's heading.

VI

And each angel had six wings: with two of them they covered their face, with two their feet and with two they would fly. They were the *s'raphim*, Hebrew for 'Burning Ones', the fire dragons and griffins derived from the Babylonian stone-temple guards. The flame-red of the Seraphim symbolized the divine love of God; the Cherubim, by contrast, were blue. In the hierarchy of angels that ringed the seat of God, they were the highest. All the others came into being in the transit from one language to another. Where the Hebrew simply spoke of an army of God, the Greek version turn it into *dynameis*: plural Powers that were then promoted to a separate category of angels, equated with two Greek words. It was Paul, in his Letter to the Ephesians, who equated this expression for military strength with two Greek words: from them in turn came in Latin the Powers and Virtues, the angels of the sun and those of Venus.

And so translations and Apocrypha write into being what was never described, and Dionysius' *Celestial Hierarchy* was what was finally needed to confer all their ranks, to clothe them in blue and to assign them to the planets, so that could they run into me here on the way home from the pub. And now I come to think about it, you can't be any further, up in the stars, than, say, half an hour's drive.

On the only stretch of road that runs straight along by the river, I sometimes turn the headlights off so that I drive for a second or two in the dark and see the earth turning towards the night. From the hill, and from the house then, the earth lies below me; the sea its stage, the stars extras, and beyond the clouds a handful of actors waiting for their cue to enter. Each one I give a different prompt: they always make a decent fist of it. In the orchestra pit between the islands the wind slowly tunes up; the beam of the lighthouse flashes the scenery before one's eyes every five seconds, but audience there is none. The rows of seats are empty. I walk through the grass; it brushes against my shoes. All is still, and I wish your voice was with me now, whispered and low so that only I could hear it. Instead the moon starts off on a soliloquy. Where it stands, stubbornly apart, is the southwest and somewhere behind is where you are, as if I only had to concentrate to see that far, peer over the curvature of the earth. But where you are it is an hour later, I only wish I knew how to catch up that hour.

Then at last I go to bed and sometimes I dream, simply because I decide I want to. In my dream I listen and now and then I hear the rustle of leaves, and wake. That whiteness shining on the wall was only the moon again, still in the midst of its soliloquy; it's skipped page after page of its script, it's already onto the next play, and the stars hurry off to find some kind of response, but that hour cannot be caught up, the revolving stage has been locked into place, the scenery is grass and trees again, and it's just your eyes there, narrow as the leaves on the blackberry bush over by the hedge, the branches tangled like the lines of your hands; there are two hands, one gives, the other holds back and I wish I could just run my hands through your hair instead and say something, the one thing you'd hear. But I am so busy searching for words, mustering my wits, that I don't even notice what a bad actor I make, and an even worse prompt.

So the night remains open, it has a fissure that is the milky way, an edge over which the light drips and into the field in front of the window, the laughter of the dawn, and it's another sleepless night, it's nearly light, there is so much time, but days and weeks won't be enough for me to discover what it would take to make you open your eyes wider. I'm nothing but a bungling fool: Apollo played by a repertory hack, who strikes a pose, draws the bow in a way he takes for suitably theatrical and shoots arrows into the night. I'm shooting arrows into the night and would sorely like to have hit a star, once at least, but the rabbits are making themselves scarce; they haven't a clue what's going on: out of nowhere it's hailing arrows into the grass, and what's more after midnight, when every respectable rabbit is busy with its rabbit business, which is after all what makes the world go round. But then suddenly there's this guy, who thinks he's a marksman, a regular *Freischütz*,

Onuphrius, patron of domestic livestock, Egyptian desert saint who fell onto all fours and crawled before the angels who came to give him Holy Communion, while huntsmen chased him with dogs, thinking him a small animal, long-haired hermit that he was, dressed only in a loincloth of leaves.

36

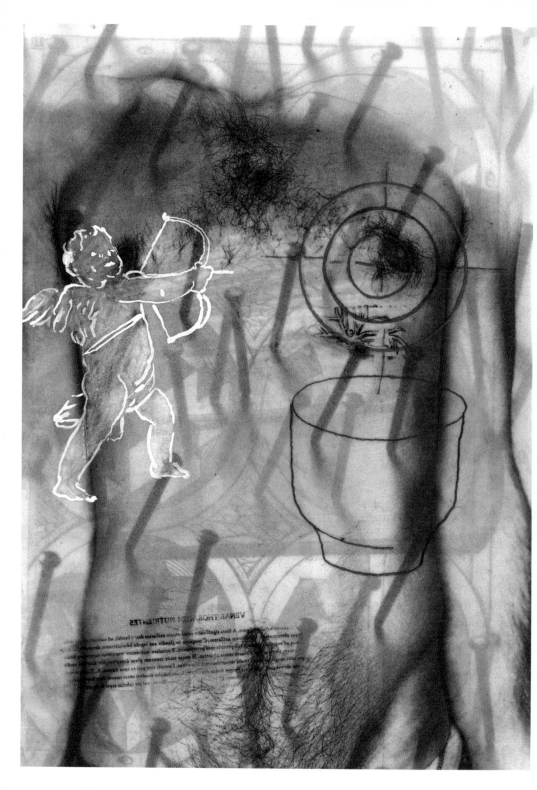

who can't hit a thing, not even from one end of the stage to the other, where this miserable dilettante seems to imagine he's some kind of Saint Sebastian, how has he got that idea, this martyr-lite, operetta clown, and anyway: he should learn to shoot first, hopefully he'll get the knack soon, hopefully the arrows in his quiver will run out, this tin-pot cupid who's holding his stomach in so as to cut a more heroic figure, and drives through the night with his eyes shut, which puts the wind up the rabbits, whose zigzagging does them no good at all, as he's just going round in circles anyway, scouring the road for the way home, home wherever that may be. Besides, he only sees it in your belly, and he'd gladly bury himself there, hold his breath and clasp you in both hands and tell you all the things you'd never believe from him: How could it come true otherwise, I ask you?

Sebastian, patron saint against religious hatred, was shot at with arrows until believed dead in the Flavian theatre; his name comes from the Greek and means 'sublime one'.

VII

Don't wonder, when of all possible corners of the earth, this morning you will receive a postcard from none other than the Lüneburg Heath. Next to the hotel there is a funeral director, a Herr Brokelmann who, in the shop next door, flogs the furniture of the deceased: a few steps further and you come to the church, and lying in front of it in the grass are three rusty bells from 1922. Between the trees, the last of the sunlight and just the start of the sky. I can still see the way you move down a catwalk, without a model's typical gait; on the balls of your feet, to be sure, but moving too much with your hips for a catwalk parade. You thrust your collar bone, your neck and head forward a touch, as if, doing that, you could be half a step faster than your shadow; your back was rounded as if you had something to hide; but that doesn't catch it quite. Afterwards it was clearer: how you sit with your arms wrapped round your knees in front of you, turn and look over your shoulder, as if in that moment you suddenly became aware of their absence, the wings that normally grow from the shoulders of angels, these pinions that always look so heavy in the oil-paintings despite the white of the feathers. But there's no doubt that the angels taught you how to laugh, though it's the tiny wrinkles at the corner of your eyes that make it true: the recording angel. The angel who lets its gaze wander just as one wants to hold it.

And I think of your laughter—as if you had stolen away out of the host of angels and did not know who of this group gathered here has been sent to fetch you back. It could be any of them, you never know. It's astonishing what you can see from the terrace here, isn't it? I'd give

Sergius and Bacchus; high-ranking officers of the Roman Guard in the interior. Sergius' martyrdom consisted of being forced to walk 18 miles alongside the Governor's carriage, wearing women's clothes and in shoes with sharp nails in as a humiliation; afterwards an angel healed his wounds.

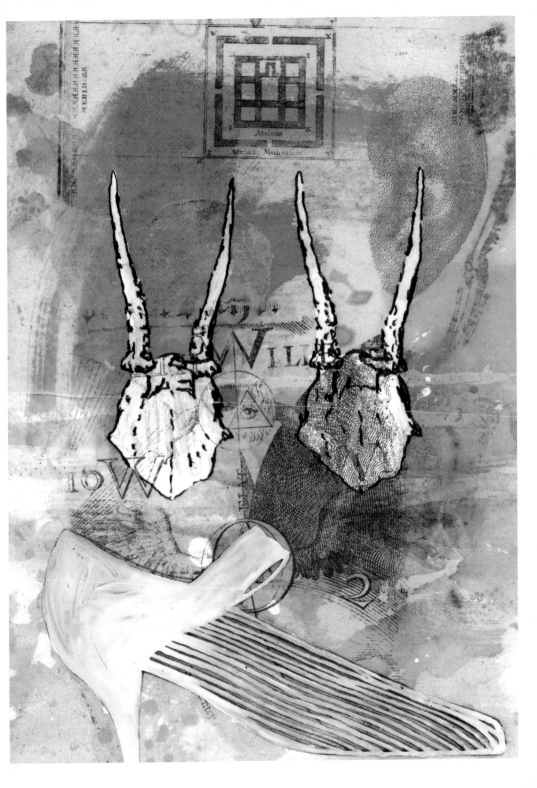

Damit Speis und Trank gedeih', saucht Pirnis Hand sie benedei'

anything to have you sitting at one of these tables close by. Then I could think what one would have to say to embarrass you. Yes, indeed.

The angel was there when I saw your back, the way you lift your shoulders when you walk, or sit down: almost as if you felt naked. It even surprised me the way the picture of an angel came to me immediately: perhaps because an angel embodies a friendlier aspect of the unapproachable. What would they enjoy hearing now, one of your kind? And what could I tell an angel, being something quite other as I am: How about 'The Tailor of Ulm' who built a flying machine and fell from the sky? Angels, angels, angels . . . I know of course, you eat like humans do, but your nourishment evaporates like dew. Anyway: I'm in Ireland until Sunday and if in the meantime you manage to find where the devil one can get a good meal there, then I would gladly invite you; *off the record*.

Pirmin of Reichenau, Irish iterant monk, Auxiliary Saint for eye troubles, attacked by worms and poisoned while eating; hideous snakes would flee before him.

VIII

Qui fecit caelos *in intellectu*: angels and men both partake equally in the heavens; they were both created in them: that is what was written by the first, and for many years, the only translator of the Areopagite, John Scottus Eriugena. But his are inverted heavens: the affirmation of man is the negation of the angel; the sublation of man is the affirmation of the angel, and vice versa. For the angel finds its form within humankind through the spirit (*intellectus*) of the angel that is in man; and man comes into being in the angel through the spirit of humankind within

him and so on and so forth for all eternity without a single
Amen being granted to us in Eriugena's scholastic per-
mutations. We are nothing but the imaginings of angels;
and angels exist only in our thoughts: that is our paradox
not theirs. *Affirmatio enim hominis negatio est angeli, negatio
vero hominis affirmatio est angeli, et vicissim.*

In the third Book of his *Divisione naturae*, Eriugena calls
the angels *mystica animali*. They exist in the depths of
nature yet never cease striving to fly, upwards, towards the
heights, unreachable even for them. Where they remain
they cover their faces with their wings and conceal their
feet from the light falling on them. I wonder whether they
cast any shadow.

      Within the figure of the angel, Eriugena
claims, the cause of all things finds expression: light. So it
follows that as an allegory the angel is that which he takes
from above and of which he speaks to himself in wonderful and inexpressible remembering, as it were an image
of the image (*imago imaginis expressa*). And if, according to
this, the angel can know what comes from above in this
way, how could one claim that he does not possess an
apprehension of what comes from below, from our realm?

In this nether realm, though, we are more than him. As humans we understand (*intelligere*) like the angel, reason like him (*ratiocinari*), have senses like animals and are like plants. It could be, someone might interject, that it is the same with angels. To such a man Scottus Eriugena would reply that the senses (*sensus*) belonging to animals can only exist in a body made of the four elements. There is no sight where there is no body; there is no hearing where there is no air; without moisture there can be no smell or taste and the absence of the earth makes the sense of touch impossible. Yet the body of an angel is pure and made of spirit (*spiritualis*) and does not have any outer senses. In humans one finds a good deal that the nature of angels cannot bear, whereas in the angel there is nothing that of its essence does not already exist in humankind. That may be its beauty. Terrible, though, is his voice; it speaks the human but promises the divine: what is terrible about an angel is his speech.

Lucernam lucubrantem a luce clarissima mundum implente: this morning I was up on Mount Gabriel. It had become cold overnight and the air was like a polished lens: the sky arched over, everything beneath folded together, even what normally remains hidden beyond the horizon. To the North the peninsulas reaching out into the sea, the upturned sediment on Hungry Hill black in the sunshine; to the East a band of cloud approaching, nothing else, only the wind over the ridge and everything filled with blue: that blue once known by the medieval painters.

Against this background I will portray you, I will sketch you from the mirror, forgoing the angel's-eye of perspective and painting you on a smooth piece of wood; and again I will wipe away the charcoal marks with the back of my hand and start over, without ever being able to capture your figure. And so I will use just this one colour to see the fire in the corner of your eyes, hear the passage of your footsteps through the air, taste on the high moor that rain you will scoop before long with both arms from the clouds, sense how the earth turns towards you, affirm you, negate you and vice versa and will be thirty saints and one for you, the one you don't yet know: Saint Never Never.

Romedius, also popularly known as Saint Never-Never originated in the family of Count of Thaur near Innsbruck, gave away all his worldly goods, and took up residence in a lonely ravine, near Tavon at Nonsberg, where he also died. In the Christian tradition, his name means 'redemption, salvation'.

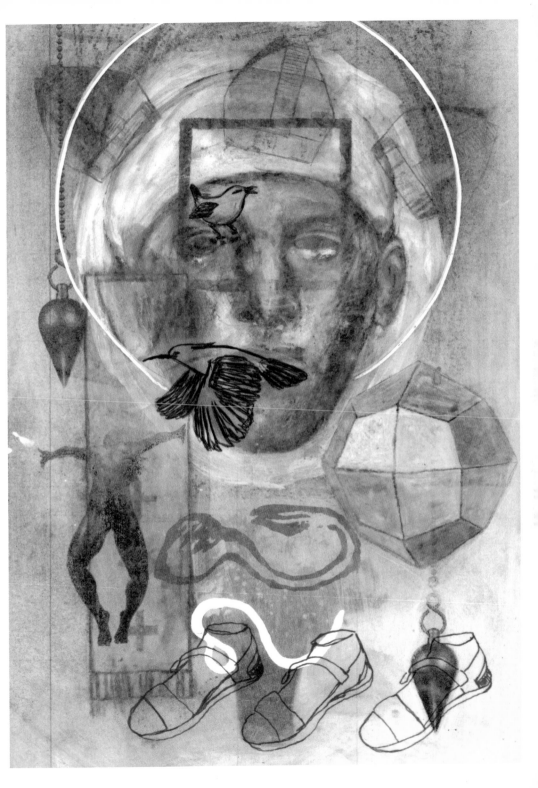

IX

But what is the gender of the *mal'ak*, the heavenly messenger? To the prophet Zechariah angels appeared carrying a vat on their back in which a female figure sat: the personification of wickedness. And as he lifted his eyes he saw two women coming towards him a wind filled their wings that looked like those of a stork, and they carried off the basket between earth and heaven, so that a temple could be built to the woman in Babylonia, the heathen home of the angels.

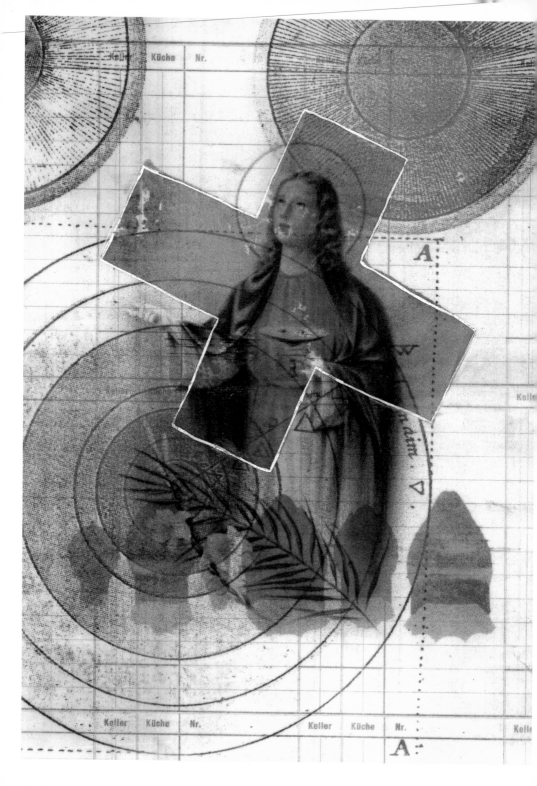

So let's get the ball rolling, crack open this vat, so I can drink to you and build a temple to you on an Italian beach. I can see you standing there now, tanned golden-brown, self-assured, swaying with your hips, a cigarette in your hand like before, but your voice half an octave deeper, personified zest for life, pure flesh and blood, my love, and the sun rolling into your lap once more. There is no more beautiful counter-image to all those northern Valkyries that transform themselves into storks simply to find a little sun in the south. But even then you didn't answer me, the post wouldn't have arrived for weeks in any case, the memory of another world, but as long as the envelope hadn't been opened, anything could have been inside; and somewhere during that long journey, somewhere in a train or a plane, the sentences might have got muddled up and might have meant something else entirely.

It's six in the evening and so warm there's a haze on the horizon; a misty white and the ferry is just arriving in the harbour at Schull, the backwash dead straight as if one had cut open a letter along the fold. It is so hot that in spite of the fog over the last few days the grass is waist-high and already brown. A crying shame: the weather like this

Lucia of Syracuse, Patron saint of repentant whores, writers and the blind (her name means 'the one filled with light'). A great beauty, she refused one proposal of marriage after another, until she was finally stripped naked and taken to a brothel; when she was martyred, she walked through the flames like a bride on her wedding day.

and I'm sitting inside writing, working at my storm, so that it blows the melancholy cobwebs out of my body: but my eye is crystal clear and with my nineteenth-century telescope I can see for miles and am looking for images. And I'm thinking about why you so much like spending time in company, why you've learnt to listen and speak so well that everything becomes an exquisite exchange. It goes from mouth to mouth, rolls off the tongue, never stays still, is always passed on; and that's why your heaven is always in a state of change and upheaval, the angels carrying mortar and bricks. You've bunked off as usual, gone swimming. And who could blame you never sticking with one thing for long, for underwater there are no directions, right and left is one and the same; there's only up when you have to come to take another breath.

Oh come on, forget all that, let's talk instead about the place you're heading for now, let's talk about the sky over Spandau and the lakes—the Müggelsee, the Müritz-see and the Nymphensee. Brandenburg that place you love above all others. In the meantime I stand here in the grass, turn to see a little breeze bending the ears of wheat, the sun still high above Mount Gabriel, and I feel safe, am light-hearted and eager about what will come. It better be angels at the very least so it all pays off. But who could have mercantile thoughts at a moment like this?

I can afford it, I have an hour in hand before you could ever arrive here, despite your best wings, and I send you my most heartfelt greetings; but tonight I will go out and of course there will be a girl sitting at the bar, you can imagine. But I won't be unfaithful to you, it's a story to carry round in one's head and that's enough. She has red hair, my love, a magnificent head of curls like yours, one that will remain unmatched in Italian iconography. They talk about Titian red; but what of Neapolitan Vesuvius red, crimson, scarlet and ruby! And I say hallelujah to that; but that's a different story.

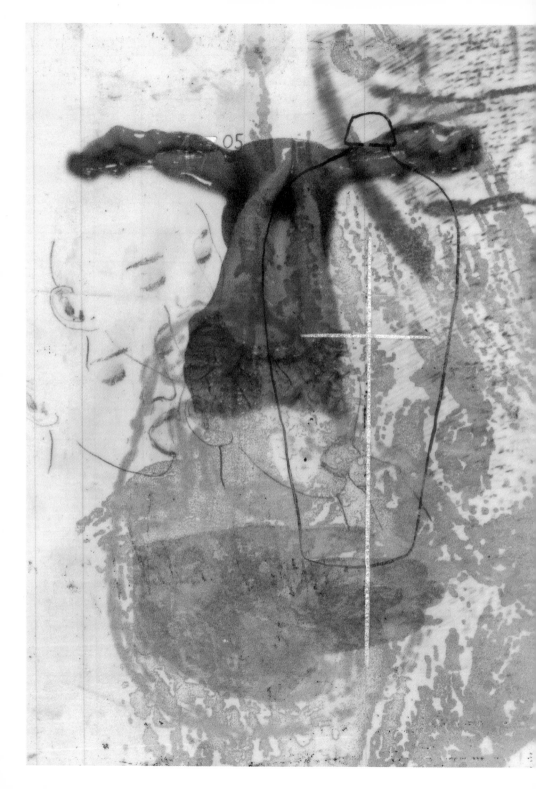

is the angel in a great rustle of sound; if it descends, the trees grow dark. Resin and honey, a swarm of bees at the bark: all the sweetness and bitterness that would be between your legs: the hairs, the roots of night. The white of the skin, the tongue that never gets beyond it, the tip writing an M in the flesh, the mouth that erases it again. Purple, the purple of a snail (of the Ophahim the fourth angel at the throne) a purple snail, *cunnus*, the tongue red in this red, its whole *lingua franca*.

Margaret of Antioch, the beautiful shepherdess was one of the virgines capitales, or four virgin martyrs, the Auxiliary saint and patron of virgins and fecundity; her name in Greek means 'pearl'.

X

But how is it that angels grow their wings? Let me tell you a story of human love, one from the time of its very beginnings. Imagine, if you will, one of those countries that has become Biblical, a village of tamped mud at the edge of one of two rivers; or maybe not, but in any case, imagine a dusty path to your house, on between the prickly pears, those Greek figs that are called torch plants because of their blooms. And don't forget that a woman was a field, a heath, a hill in the thicket of bushes, in the middle of which there was a clearing, a copse to honour the gods, so that the man would make this earth fruitful.

Petat pussumi was what they called the ritual according to which a woman received her beloved in Mesopotamia: the 'revelation of the concealed'. Before she allowed him into the house, she would wash with the water from tamarisk leaves and soapwort with a few drop of olive oil to make the skin silky smooth. Then the hair was removed from the nipples and with great care from the labia, from the anus to the clitoris, that *dubdub* bird in its furrow that some people think is simply the roller bird. Those of us who know better translate it as a species of Lepidoptera or, in German, the 'nocturnal moth', that hides during the day under a bush. That is where the wings of the angels come from, from this moth and the way it emerges from the cocoon into the imago in order to become visible.

Hot beeswax was probably what they used; the pain involved, as with the purification ritual as a whole, has a symbolic function. It was meant to expunge the memories of any previous lover. The faintly reddened skin would be rubbed with an ointment of wild chamomile and other flowers.

Maria Magdalena, patron of repentant sinners, the de-flowered, hairdressers and the makers of powder and perfume; depiction with the risen one in *Noli me tangere.*

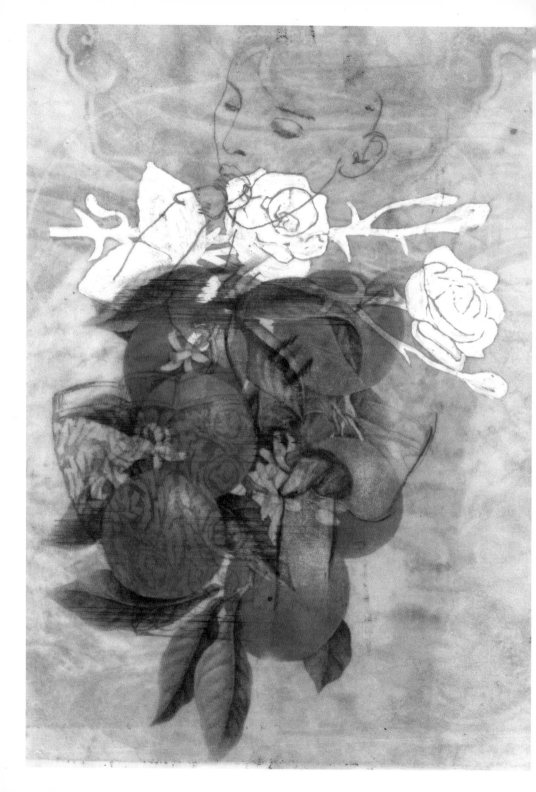

And as long as the condition of being in love lasted, for that time the woman's 'nether mouth' would remain open, kept free 'for laughter'—*ina muhhi siahi*, as the custom was also called at the time of King Ashur bel kala (1074–1057 BCE). This phrase not only indicates the desire that takes hold of the body and the familiar deep laughter that comes from it, but also, in its second meaning, the opening and closing of butterfly wings.

The Cherubim, as you know, was a Babylonian angel. And you know too that he decorated himself with tiny lapis lazuli beads round his neck, double rows of pearls across his breast and golden bands round his wrist. After he has bathed and been anointed, he lines his eyes with antimony and coats his wings with an aphrodisiac called *kurgarru*. And with this a flying creature of the night becomes one of the day, one with blue wings like the Polyommatus eros, the Eros Blue butterfly. If you take it between your fingers, it leaves a residue of silvery dust on the tips.

And the menfolk? I hear you ask. The Indian fig (*Cereus n. catacea*) also has a second common name, on account of its fruit: the dildo tree. Go on laugh, for it's a roundabout route to get there. Man's weakness is

Dorothea of Caesarea, patron of gardeners, who in the midst of the harshest winter, sent her headdress to an unbeliever, a writer, carried by an angel; it was filled with oranges and roses.

a grave one; they try to disguise it behind a plethora of indecipherable names. There is a winding path between the hills that are dotted with torch plants to the *arbor vitae*, which men, willing though weak, could only depict with the votive offering of a *penis succedaneus*. Already in Babylonian times it was fashioned out of sandalwood, ivory, horn, or, rather more candidly, out of wax. The Greeks called it *olisbos*, though it is not known what the word actually means; for the Romans is was *phallus* or *fascinum*, which is less difficult to decipher; though where the *lingam* or *rin-no-tam* of the far East come from, nobody knows. The French are just as guarded about how they arrived at the word *godemiche*, though the English admit quite candidly that the term *pillicock* or *pintle* simply comes from the quantities of beer consumed in their public houses. So we are left to turn to the Italians who shortened the *passatempo* or *diletto* to the dildo we know today. That one could then follow the loop back to the Indian fig might be explained by the fact that in Italy anything to do with love is named for fruit or fish; though that might be a wee bit far-fetched.

Digressions, I know, on no account any further digressions; and I press a kiss onto your mouth with my hands, take you into my arms, though that's as far as it goes for tonight, for writing is a thing unto itself, it needs a little . . . but if you close your eyes . . . I am promised all the houris of the Prophet.

XI

Before Muhamad fell into frenzy, he heard the humming of bees and the tinkling of a bell; then the archangel Gabriel appeared before him and dictated the surahs of the Koran; but Muhamad refused to recite them back to the angel and record them until Gabriel, in his anger, caught him by the throat and began to strangle him (some say with a silken scarf, on which letters were drawn). Of course no one believed his writings to be more than poetry written by an epileptic fool: every poet had a personal daemon in those days. It became a religion only when it was accepted that God was the source of its inspiration, not Iblis (a corruption of *diabolus*) or a djinn. At that point poetry became profane, but not for long: as it couldn't make do without metaphysical legitimation, the angels crept back into literature.

And: no, I am not writing for writing's sake; no, if my letters were in any way beautiful, they were so only on account of you; no, they are not complete in themselves; all they do is beg for the answer and conceal best they can the question (they tiptoe in stealth as I know they are trespassing on your territory). No, your cheeks were so warm that it felt as if I had woken up next to you; no, there is nothing that could possibly dis-appoint you from the rank of the angels; no, the Amores will never run out of arrows, although I make a rather unholy Sebastian; and no, the angels will not wear themselves out with words; writing to you brought at least a few hours relief, then you started up again humming in my ears.

Yes, it is the before and after that matter, but above all the now: now in this train where I'm writing this on my knees (keeping the paper still is nigh-on impossible with the train winding round all those bends and curves). God, how long have I been waiting for a

Bonaventura, patron of silk-makers, honorary title *Doctor Seraphicus*, who saw shadow (*umbrae*) behind things, traces (*vestigia*) and images (*imagines*); and an angel appeared to place a host on his tongue and thus to loosen it.

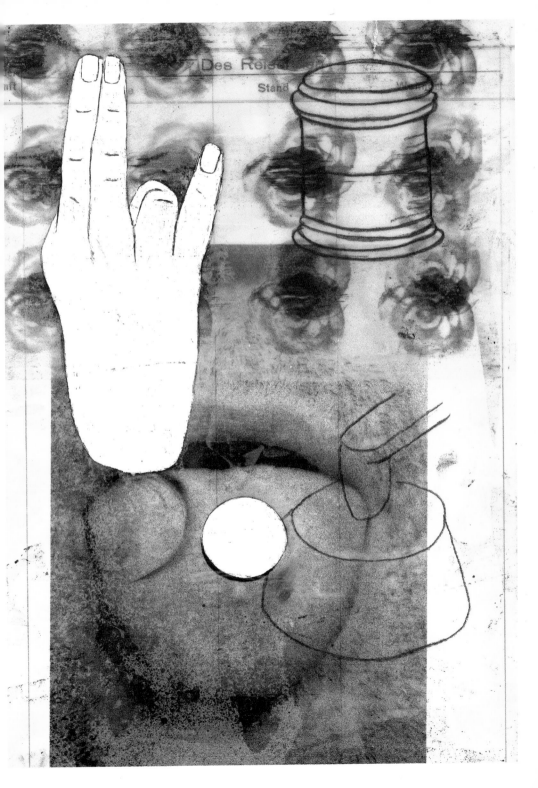

letter from you; how long it all takes with those days of
Catholic repentance and prayer over the last few weeks.
Days of fasting, Ramadan to say the least, and three times
a day I go to look at the mailbox, expecting with every
day that goes by for you to say something like: *well, thank
you, I'm rather embarrassed to say this, but* . . . But the box is
always empty, the train winds through the mountains,
tonight I'm giving a reading where I will only see you
sitting somewhere in the front few rows, feel my throat
tightening, getting stage-fright.

            I fled, and no wonder,
with all those tides and the pull of the moon; you do the
only sensible thing and take refuge 3,000 feet above sea
level. I hiked up into the mountains only to come straight
back down, go home so I could write to you in the
evening, and how I wished I could have been at sea with
you; wished I could have spent the whole summer with
you before it even began; I wished, I wished . . . and all
these letters that were only written to hurry on ahead of
an angel and try to anticipate it. Hopeless sceptic that I
am, expecting only silence in return, as befits an angel in
its planetary orbit, its ballet on my fingertips, while one
day after the next runs away from me. Sleepwalking. Like
a fool, torn in two, dogs at his heels, a rose in his hand,

butterflies before his nose, one foot hovering over the abyss. And the only thing that holds me up in the air is my longing (and I trust in angels without believing in them for a moment). It's almost a miracle.

XII

Hermes, god of thieves, the one angel before there were angels, it's his silence that falls into my letters and robs me of words; that's when my angel is crossing the room. He's having a fine old time of it, him and his crew, smashing glasses against the wall: tonight the angels are out for a spree, they have sneaked away from their troop, gone AWOL. Three-quarter moon again, almost a whole coin: one that has slipped through the hole in the seam of my trouser pocket. The sky an artifice. The gaze wandering off while thinking through what can be thought through. Japanese characters in a room across the way, on the other side of the street: a storage room for cardboard containers and boxes, the light still on. The moon above my left shoulder, half of Cassiopeia bright against the neon.

The things the letters avoid. The frame, with the grid stretched over it, the abscissa: literally, that which is cut off. How can I know that what I write to you is not projection? At this point the only thing I trust is longing; it's all that allows me to relate to things, to their reality that always retreats from me; always a hand's breadth beyond what the fingertips can reach. Syzygy: Now what does this word mean? Why did it just come into mind? It must be something astronomical.

All of it words, simply words. And so much I want to tell you that would depend on the silences in between, on your voice, your eyes. It has still has to be sketched out, my fingers slowly following the line of your ankle, running along your heel, as you climb up the heavenly ladder again, freckle by freckle. But that was when angels still went on foot and the world was not yet too heavy for them.

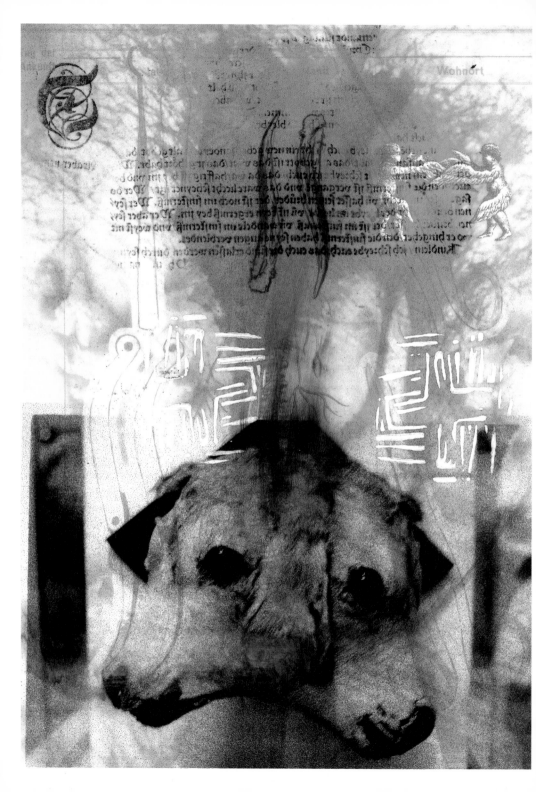

Addendum

is the half of life that one only half-remembers. Ever since that Mayday I have been wide awake, sleep scarcely more than four hours at a stretch; that must be the meaning of this heathen ritual.

Crispin and Crispinian, Roman brothers, who were flayed alive. They turned to the true faith in the Middle Ages, became shoemakers and through this played a significant part in Christianity reaching Osnabruck.

XIII

And back to Hermes, who weighs the souls of the dead on his scales before he leads them down into the underworld realm of his brother Hades: *mene tekel u-parsin,* weighed and found wanting. So, my angel. So, the lighthouse on Fastnet Rock like a pedestal for seaborne angels, on which they alight, imitating the gulls. So, yes exactly so. And what can he write to you, Simeon the Stylite, who stands all day on his column, erect, staring into the sun and turning with it, to keep the world in balance? Let me at least build him a railing for the stormy nights, the nights of exhaustion, when his whole body aches, so that he doesn't fall. I'll just fetch a few planks and nail together a makeshift balustrade. After all, he's one of your orders, a high-ranking soldier in your host. Let it all come down, crashing over him.

So, angel. There are many women and men who love the bells you have fastened in the rain for them, and many of them that wanted you, simply found what they'd always wanted, again and again. Maybe, just let it stand for a moment, to cover for the things that I will never understand. You don't answer, you've never answered. Light again, its tongue licking the rocks. Let's say there is someone writing you letters and the letters come from far, far away: semaphores, signal lights, beacons, just for you to see how far off the horizon is and where at eye-level it ends. And it's reassuring, the indecisiveness of it all is reassuring, and that there is no need for more. Unless the letters stop. And then it's a maybe again—maybe again. But then you'd have to know what it is you have to ask. But there are no answers with the letter; none in them; the letters being just an invitation. That invitation was delivered long ago.

Thomas Aquinas, patron of pencil-makers and book-sellers; Auxiliary Saint against storms; rejected all high office in order to preach his works from the pulpit. Depicted with a dove that flies from his mouth, girded with a mystical belt by two angels; occasionally also with fools' bells.

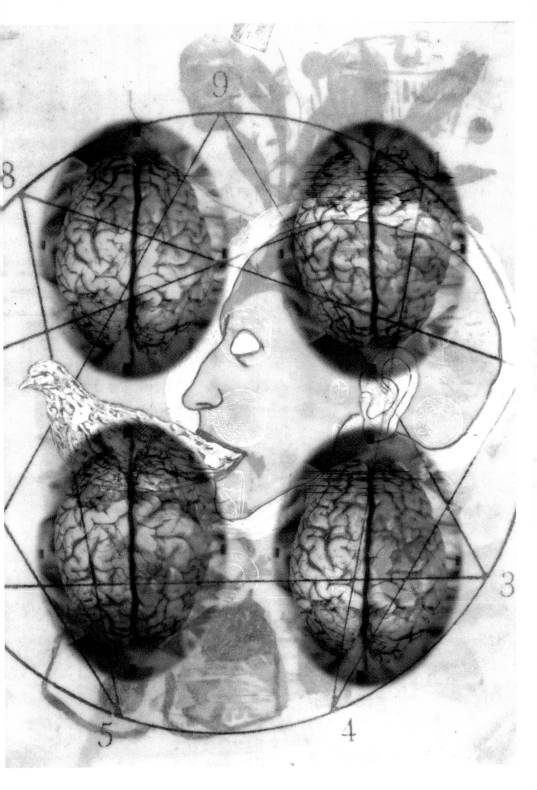

An invitation you decline like degrees from a longitude to mark a position. But what do I know anyway, being neither boatswain nor helmsman?

The ships are coming in with nightfall, into the leeward of Cape Clear. The lighthouse will start its fire long before the astronomical twilight. But don't trust the lighthouse. Rather it's a fireship, coming in to anchor before the dawn. And the beach full of clocks made of paper, cardboard and wood (I like this image) for the solstice, that people set alight and send out on the water. And the tides turn; they don't wait for a ship. So, angel. So. What else could I tell you that you'd have to find out for yourself? And the view is as clear, you see as far, as the crow flies. I think of you, still and quiet. This much I have promised, as a pledge, in the perfect tense of writing letters to you. Now it's up to you. Come. And if you don't, it doesn't.

The chalk wall of the house over on Horse Island lights up for an instant, always the first time, the first time over and again. That's the way the bay takes form, draws silhouettes, tongues of land, as if breaking into speech, tips almost touching each other, a hand, an arm, the slope of

Mount Gabriel. Well, in words, at least. Everything else is different, is real, a mouthful of air.

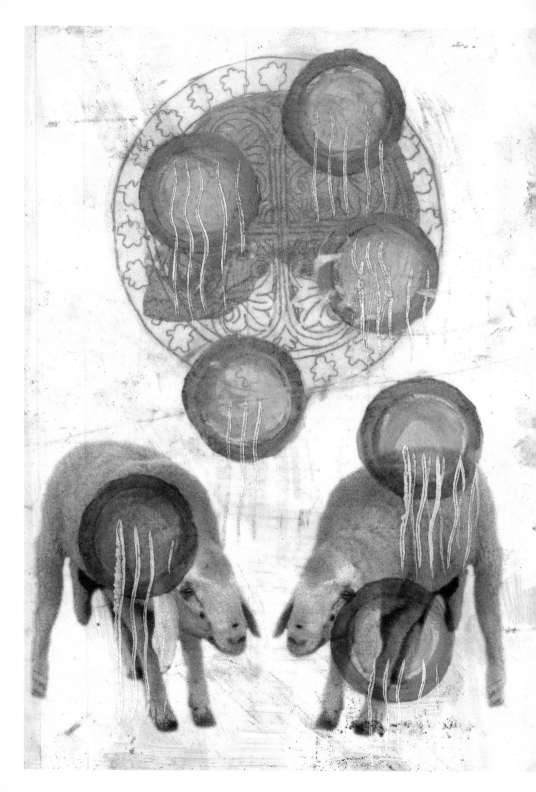

Clement I, Pope,
author of Letter to
the Corinthians;
patron of stone-
cutters, because
he caused a clear
stream to gush
from the rocks of
a quarry where
the workers were
dying of thirst. On
account of this he
was thrown into
the Black Sea
with an anchor
round his neck.

XIV

And the firmament drew in and descended, black clouds lying thick over the sea; and something floated on the wings of the wind and had the body of a lion, the legs of a bull and a human head. There approached a Babylonian angel; one of those who intercede for humankind with the gods. The Greeks pronounced the Akkadian *krb* ('bless', 'pray') as *grypos*; the Romans as *gryphus,* only we have the name through the Brothers Grimm as 'Griffin'. He revealed himself to the Egyptians under another name, as *ssp-nh* (which means 'living image'). See, you can hardly pronounce it. Nor could the Greeks. What they heard in those hard consonants was something that reminded them of their word *sphiggein* ('choke', 'fetter') and that's how they finally came to understand the dark side of this angel: the Sphinx. Not that I'm Oedipus with an answer to its riddle; and I only have an extra leg in the morning.

The stars were out last night, the whole Babel of the heavens, the wind sharp and cold, and all the figures drawn on the firmament, but I was blind: there were just lights before my eyes that wouldn't cohere to recognizable shapes. I came back alone yesterday, came back to demons, ghosts in the house, spirits sleeping next to me and waking with me, succubae, Liliths and whatever all these nightmares are called: I don't care. I'll smoke them out with sulphur. Makes me bad company tonight; and even worse these past days. Perhaps I shouldn't have waited for the tide to come; I should just have set sail, running before the wind instead of tacking as now. But I don't think I could have outrun things, even with the best seamanship, hove-to would have been about my limit. But I should have tried. Instead of that, I'm back at my desk again. And I'm sitting here thinking about why, and what it is in me,

Christopher, patron of sailors and raftsmen, Auxiliary Saint against floods, carried pilgrims across the water.

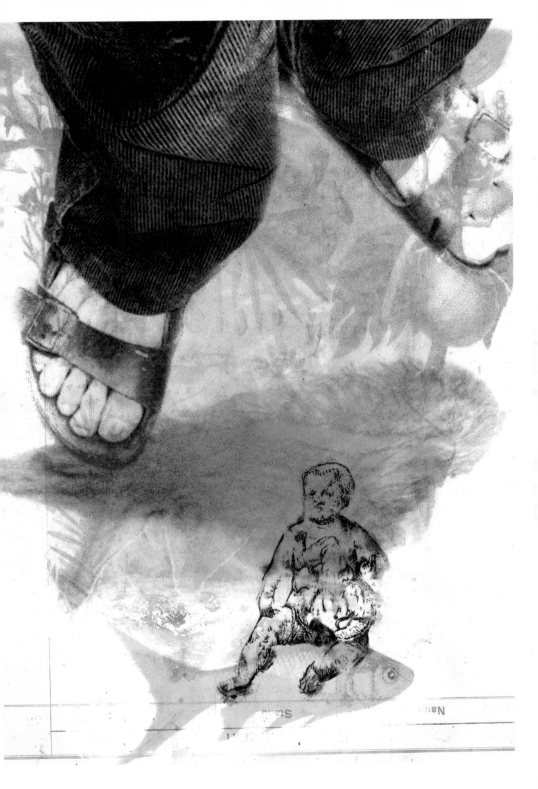

and if I've only managed to avoid it by talking to an angel about angels: from heaven to the earth the angels fall down dead. Seems that all I've ever wanted from them is my own private salvation. But salvation from what? And now they are all coming back, all of them with your face, and with every phrase they get closer and finally they are standing beside my bed and have no answer. And I ask them for forgiveness, deliverance, oblivion, God knows, he invented them all—to hell with him.

The beam of Fastnet Rock passes across the wall every five seconds, too fast for a heartbeat, too slow for a breath; there are two lives sketched there, separate, irreconcilable, unlike the lighthouse beams, two parallels that meet at one point, even if it is only to do a favour for the eye. Still I don't know why or how; just know it somewhere in the core of a self that I suppose must be mine. It caught me unexpected, unforeseen; maybe because I confided in you, trusted you with so much, that somewhere in the midst of this long confession, the Mephisthophelean truth slipped out. And now I don't know whether to trust this devil, or what I should do with his insinuations.

True: what would fit nicely with this moral catechism is remorse; but I don't feel even a trace. Only the stabbing pain in the side, a stitch in the ribs, just as HE once felt it. I'd do penance, if I knew what for (all this Catholic vocabulary is leading me onto thin ice and the fact I've always been bad at metaphysics). So I'll fight it out with myself, or whatever you call it when it has nothing to do with a struggle, only with weakness. And you not at all. An immaculate angel, having come down to earth, to the waters, and me just seeing chimera, me standing on the shore; the harpies have me their claws in me, throttle me, them and all the other abominable monsters of my own imagining. So I will be steadfast, and offer my liver for them to eat. And not being a god, not even a demi-god, I'll just have to wait until they've devoured the rest of me too.

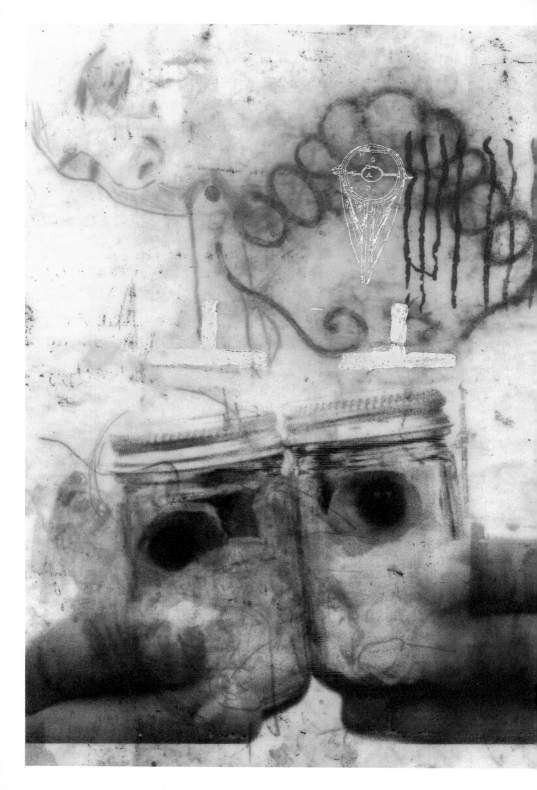

Odilia, depicted in
the white gown of
her order carrying
a book on which
lie two eyes (born
blind, she received
her sight on being
baptized).

XV

On the fifth day of the fourth month in the thirtieth year (though I'm older and it's already August), the sky opened for Ezekiel alone. High above the heads of the Cherubim, the 'Never sleeping', he saw the crystalline sphere of light; they had spread their wings, one touching the next. Two of the wings covered their body and Ezekiel heard the swish as they closed, it was like the roar of the ocean.

I, on the other hand, am just thankful that you don't bring the seven heavens crashing down upon my head and seven seas up to my neck. The weather has been good today, hot; it's a shame to be at my desk again, but I did drive down to Baltimore (the Irish one that the American one is named after) and ate there, the sun in the window and it made me quiet. And I've decided that the world is neither flat nor round, nor is it for me to wrench from its orbit. Instead it's a cone and I'm trying to stand on the point, much like you angels do all the time with a jar of water or some such on your head to keep balance: I can only keep balance as long as I concentrate and don't think of anything else. Out there in the open air, on the grass, turning slowly on my own axis. Like one of those figures on a glockenspiel: the hour chimes and out they come, wound up and performing their couple of tricks; but the mechanism is somehow stuck, the springs are broken, don't ask me how or why. Then again, some days I feel free like I've nothing to lose, a dizzy feeling (I'm exaggerating), and then some sad dog creeps up on me, wheedling and rubbing round my knees.

That afternoon I did nothing but sketch figures in the air that was like glass, with the light everywhere, even when the fog rolled in from the evening. Ah, my angel, you should have known me as I was before, then I could have

Valerie of Limoges; was converted after her betrothal and insisted on virginity whereupon her disappointed bridegroom had her beheaded; angels appeared to bear her to heaven.

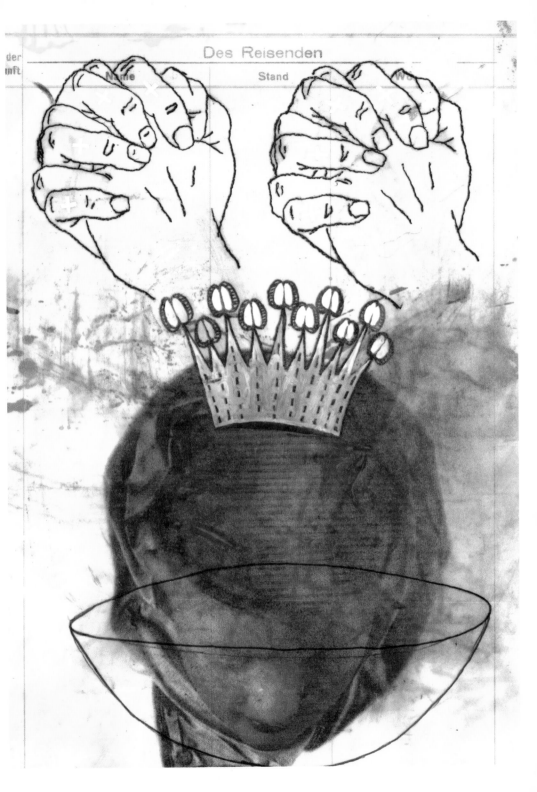

brought off the tricks as I always did, but today it doesn't look good for gentlemen vagabonds, hotel tricksters and conmen, of the sort I would have liked to be. Not that I haven't enjoyed it and everyone around me too, but perhaps it was only done for the applause. Nothing to do with you, though, my angel, don't be mistaken: just the circus pony tired of the same old rounds while the clowns clown, the fire-eaters swallow their turpentine and the sword-eaters choke. But there I am thinking in allegories again; they provide such a picturesque backdrop for one's poor self, oh my! In a fool's game, no one fools the fooler. And I hope you are well and that everything comes back to you. And meanwhile I am setting the fire in the hearth, I'm about to tear the pages of the newspaper and the fog is coming up the hill as if it were going to snow (which it never does here).

There was an article about an orchid-thief and my eye fell on the word trickster, and then, a page further on, two words in the margin on the left: 'haunted house'. That conjured up something indistinctly, a woman looking back over her shoulder perhaps, long hair falling down— or perhaps it's just the sound of these words—the way the cheeks hollow out when one says them, deep like a well, but the sound when the stone falls into the water is soft: haunting. The more I think about it, the more I like the word, its ideas: something for an orchid-thief. A panama on his head. What would he look like here in his linen suit, out on the moors in the pouring rain? It will be a long time before I can be of service to the Amores again. My jacket, the cufflinks and the Italian shoes, none of them fit me any longer, the roses have wilted. I can't find the old charm, don't know how to turn it on: don't know what I'm about. And what kind of visitation is this anyway? A sly one at the hands of the Fates or a violent one courtesy of Nemesis and the harpies? Sisyphus must have been the first of my kind, more of a man than me and unholier by far.

XVI

This letter is a last, very last, etymological gloss from my angelology, to tell you what you are for me, here on earth, since there's no other place in the world. And with that I return to Classical times and the only reflection of heaven that I can find anywhere. The Greeks called the blue-grey of the ocean in the twilight *glaucos*: the light that seemed to come from nowhere, the shimmer rising up from the depths, the currents visible between the islands, the glint of slate when wet, the light breaking on it; the glimmer of leaves caught by a gust of wind and

TAB. V.

By this means they are Combined.

Here is Labour & there is Rest.

turned over (the glistening white of eyes in the night beneath the trees, that was the owl: *glaux*).

The moon is back again: in that same place, where I wrote it into the perfect fairy copy of the first letter. The dull beams of light penetrate the darkness, pretty much like always; and as it rises, the colour changes from a dull yellow to white. I'm stopping over a couple of nights here in Switzerland and the expanse of the Lake Zurich lies before me, black as molasses, the waves as if buoyed by their own weight. Capricorn to the West, over the line of the hill. And I think now I can also tell when you take refuge behind your mask—your mask of mulberry wood—when you breathe in, the vowels of the first word scarcely audible and then everything after follows that curve: a little embittered. Do angels have free will? Theirs is a long night.

I won't say what I'd like to; I'll carry on writing in the dark, it's light enough to see the shadow of my hand and the pencil against the paper, a velvety blue. And there's a spot in this completely still water, a broad ring that forms and expands and reflects the moon. I hear cows lowing from over by the beehives. I chew and spit; the wax on one side and the honey on the other, before

Romuald of Camaldoli, known for his itinerant life and his life as a hermit, in which he sought to atone for his previous life until angels showed him the ladder ascending to heaven.

winter draws in. Now I know too why it is you never answered—that way you just sink deeper inside me. Let me kiss your neck and bid you goodnight. Summer is turning over on its cushion; I wish you good night, my angel, good night. No, not yet. I'll stay looking out of the window a while longer. And wake up again early, a half-sentence already forming in my head. Half the lake now silver.

That afternoon after I'd visited the church and came back to the hotel, I saw a tourist steamer go past. I recall from my Greek that *naus* is a ship, *nos* a temple, and the two come together in the Middle Ages to become *navis*: nave. But why should that be? Perhaps on account of the water, the reflections dazzling your eyes; the sheen on the waves that lap the shore when the light falls through the clouds and the water begins to retreat. An angel is nothing but the personified meaning of the questions we ask.

Ernst of Neresheim: when his ship arrived in the Holy Land, during the Crusades, he fell into the hands of the Saracens and was martyred in Mecca when his innards were torn from his body with a winch and reel; and the moon arose honey-yellow.

XVII

I am flying towards you. Or away from you, who
could say for sure? But on the way from the airport to
Piraeus I finally hit upon a way of grasping you in age-
old, heathen terms. The ships and temples are part of it.
According to the sources, it was a certain Naos who
brought the Eleusinian Mysteries to Akkadia on the
instructions of the Delphic oracle. He sealed the mystery
of light in amphorae and carried them by ship from one
shore to the other across the sea to Crete. And years later
they named a sea-god after that light, one who was

renowned for his amorous adventures: Glaucus, the lost son of the Cretan King who had built the labyrinth. And there we are back to the whys and wherefores and what it is that connects them both.

In order to discover the fate of his son who had suddenly vanished from the face of the earth, the King consulted the oracle who told him this: that whoever could find the correct simile for the fateful birth that had just befallen his house, would be the one to find his son. The birth was that of a new born calf belonging to the King's herd, a bull calf that changed colour three times a day, from white to red and then to black. The simile that was finally found was a ripening mulberry: the sun. And how it rises above the corners and walls of a maze that is also mine. And there it was that the son was finally discovered, down in the subterranean vaults of the labyrinth; he had fallen into a vat of honey and was dead, but was then brought back to life.

In the gloom the gold gathers light against the coming of night. Words, nothing but words, you see; the necessity of angels consists in being a metaphor for what is not revealed; the light that cannot be named; already halfway

110

to the darkness of the solar eclipse that will happen soon:
the original meaning of *mal'ak* was shadow-side of God,
the dark side that he turns towards humankind.

Saint Blaise of
Sebastea, Saint of
wind and weather,
patron of candle-
sellers and wax-
makers, became
the Auxiliary Saint
against fish bones
stuck in the
throat, after he
saved a boy from
choking.

XVIII

And I promised you the night. And still haven't delivered the heavens, still haven't invented the constellations anew for you. I'm sitting on the other side of the bar, head in my hands: longing on its own isn't enough, not from so far away, and not when you sit there and lean back in your chair in your quad, run your hand through your hair and then stretch out your arm to pluck the distances from the constellations. You drink too much, look at me hardly at all, and only out of the corner of your eye, and what's written in your face I dare not say. I have a contract with my angels and I intend to fulfil it. But how? With a borrowed pencil and a story written on an accountant's pad? I'll wait for you until all the orders are in and time is called, and I'll use that time to prepare my words. And even though my drinks are all being paid for, the moon comes, from far away, over the white plastic tables and chairs, the mole in the harbour, through the trees, along the sides of the promenade. And I speak you into the darkness, read you from your lips and have nothing to go on but the stories of a boy who at first was called Anthedon.

He fell into a vat of honey, but was recovered, as I've already told you. It was pitch black in the vaults where they placed his lifeless body together with a certain diviner who had been the one to think of the mulberry simile. Now it was expected that he would restore the boy to life with his magic arts, but he had no idea how. The only thing he did was to tread on a snake and kill it as he was pacing up and down in the darkness. But then he saw how a second snake crept forth carrying a herb in its fork-tongued mouth and touched the knotted body of the dead snake; and lo, it was immediately restored to life and with it Anthedon.

Peregrine Laziosi; joined the Servite Order in Siena and distinguished himself for the zeal of his prayer and repentance. Legendary is his conversion of a whore, on whose account he rolled naked in hot sand until his legs were bleeding. He was buried under a mulberry tree.

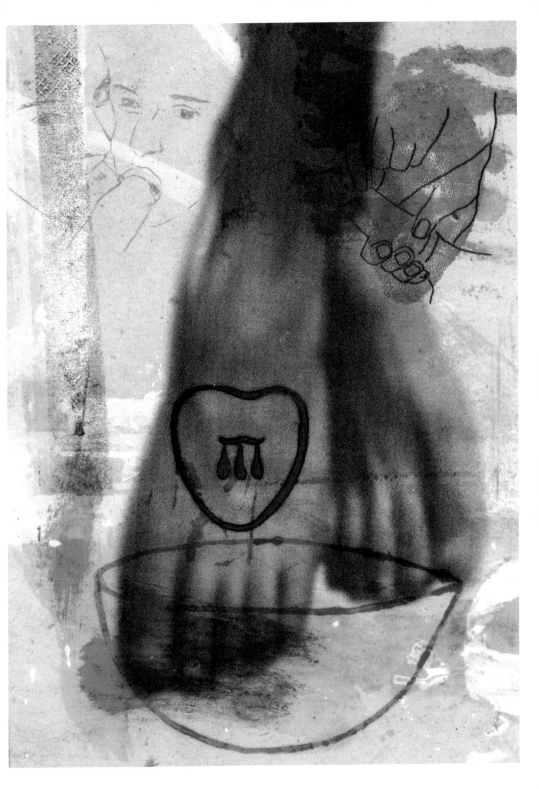

Fig. II

He grew up to be a man; and from that day forth always had a liking for things that gleamed and shifted and were smooth and loved nothing more than to travel out on the high seas. Once, however (and its always this once that saps the courage I need simply to come over and join you) he brought his boat ashore on a patch of seagrass and began to unload the fish he had caught; scarcely had he thrown them into the grass than they came back to life and leapt back into the sea. And as he jumped into the water in disbelief and began to swim after them, a transformation came over him; unawares, he turned into the sea-god Glaucus.

Jonah, Old Testament Prophet, received the command from God to go to the sinful city of Nineveh. He did not obey and fled to Tarshish. The ship got into distress, the sailors threw him into the sea, he was swallowed by a great fish and three days later spat out again on dry land. Depicted sitting in the shade of a kikayon; he became bald in the belly of the fish.

One of the hundred daughters of Poseidon, Glauce, fell in love with him when she saw him swimming in the water and called him to come to her on shore. But as he approached she was horrified and shrank from him: he had a beard as green as algae, a torso blue as the sea and his body ended in a fish tail. Just like the intransigence of land and water, so she stood implacable and summoned him, across the water line and up onto the beach; and he crawled forwards on his elbows, dragging his body, flapping with his tail, gasping for air: a ridiculous creature that she wanted nothing to do with.

What else could he do but seek refuge far away? And he found it somewhere deep in the Mediterranean, close to the island belonging to the magical Circe, who when she set eyes on him slipped into the water and coupled with him. It restored, as it were, his male pride, but as always that was not enough: he longed for his Glauce and made the mistake of telling Circe. She said nothing and let him depart; but her jealousy knew no bounds. The next time Glauce came down to the seashore to bathe, picking her way gingerly across the sharp edges of the lava with her bare feet, until she stood hip high in the sea and was scooping water up over her breasts, Circe took her revenge. She covered her legs with pelt; her feet became paws; her buttocks became dog's heads that bared their teeth between her thighs. And thus Glauce became the siren Scylla who would bare her breasts like a ship's figurehead to the sailors as they passed and lure them into her cave, where the bones of her deluded lovers still lie bleaching in the sun.

The reflection of the light on the grass and the waves becoming spray, the crowns of foam dispersed by the wind: a story of the sea. And me, by no means the patron saint of mariners. Besides: what have the angels got to do

with this? They are lost on these unchristian shores. Do I
pray to you? I prithee. And pay and leave.

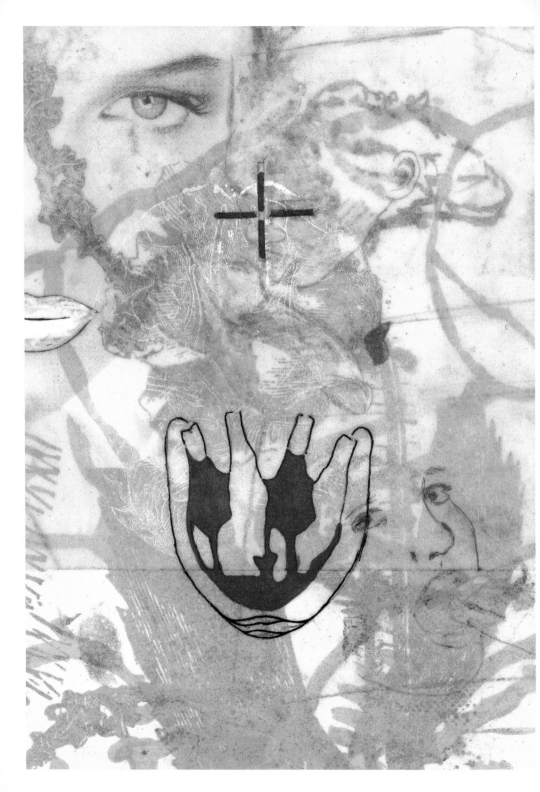

is the night, attached for you here, after the flight back to Ireland. The bells ringing vespers and with the star that is morning and evening at once, the whole story begins again in the East: the Ishtar of the two streams, Aphrodite born in the Greek sea, the urban Roman Venus, fickle and moody, as only a woman can be. I know you will argue it's not true, because you have to, but what good will it do? I look for you in everything and always see you on another table, hair swept up off your face, a classic sixties beauty, high cheekbones, a trace of bitterness round the mouth, while the evening lies over the sea, *des yeux glauques*; it spreads and, with the incoming squalls, turns invisibly to night. The night by day that will bring these letters to a close.

Gemma Galgani, lat. *gemma*, precious stone, known as the Daughter of Passion. In 1899 she manifested the stigmata, in 1900 the marks of the crown of thorns and in 1901 those of the flagellation. When she was sanctified, all the bells of Rome sounded.

XIX

But how to imagine the heaven of the saints at the end of all this? Just like the prophet Ezekiel before him, Scottus Eriugena also saw a storm wind coming from the South, a huge cloud of blazing flame that illuminated the darkness like gold. And in the midst of it were four angels and each of them had four wings. Each of them stared into one of the four corners of the wind and yet stood touching one another with the very tips of their wings; and flames darted between them from the braziers of the heavens, night torches, blazing bolts of fire. Like a rainbow appearing in the clouds, this was the vision of the glory of God. And as Scottus beheld this vision he fell to the ground and understood. Being an Irishman he seldom had to interpret the flight of a bird, let alone an angel, across the blue of the sky; he more commonly scanned for the movement of weather fronts across the island. A cloud-watcher, that is what he was, one of the *neladoir*.

From the darkness of the clouds came the light and it broke forth like the new year that began with the equinox when people lit fires and counted the days from nightfall. But that was in a time in which Lugh was still celebrated at the highest god; Lord of iron, fire and the arts, the god of that light that gave being to all; and it was also then that the wife of the sun gave her name to Ireland: Erin.

The mystery of light remained in Ireland until his epoch; in his monastery Scottus found numerous accounts of solar eclipses dating back to the fifth century when angels grew their wings. Year upon year itinerant monks like Scottus himself left the monastery to submit themselves to the martyrdom of the continent; they brought scripture and culture with them and became the teachers of the Carolingians.

So it came to pass that he was at the court of Charles the Bald, at the time of the solar eclipse of the ninth century and saw petals opening and closing again and birds going to sleep. In the scrolls of the Byzantine Church Fathers, he discovered the Neoplatonic tradition and learnt that the light and ore of his own universe was also already part of their world. As one of the few still able to read Greek, he translated the Areopagite and so prepared the spheres of the universe for Dante's *Divine Comedy*.

What John Scottus, who was named Eriugena because he was born on Erin, discovered turned the world for him into a theophany. In the creation of light, he wrote, God also creates himself; God is in man and man is in God, just as the wind begins to glow in the One Light and the iron glows in the One flame. And all things that are, are light. Light is all that is manifest; its rays break, separate, disperse until they become shade and darkness and this darkness is the matter that all things are made of: *omnia quae sunt, lumina sunt*.

When the clouds part, the light breaks across the hills covered with broom; a fat light that drops onto the grass like honey, as sweet as the aftertaste of those things that are.

The wind hardly makes an impression, at least not this morning. At low-tide Roaringwater Bay is like a mirror, half-green and half-tarnished, right out to Cape Clear, where the first Irish church stands. Streaks of wind move between Carbery's Hundred Isles of Baltimore up to Mizen Head; the whole Southwest.

And the Atlantic begins out there at Fastnet Rock; it's a cathedral cupola and a bell tower, a closed fist against the cliffs and the lighthouse is an index finger, or whatever the light chooses at that moment. Sometimes it spreads its fingers for a moment, cleaves the clouds and that window over on Horse Island bursts into flame from the sun and burns. Then the clouds of rain drifting inland leach the colours away and the earth swallows them. The sky lifts, a cumulus like a medieval flat map on which the latitudinal lines expand and distort until they become a mammatus. And as long as the sun remains hidden in the clouds, I shall have time for these lines. It is sliding high into the heavens and a sheen lies on the waters, so that one would need a different language in order to be able to describe the shimmering matt, the lustre mirrored by the light on the sea, glimmering like ash leaves or the pale flash of the underside of bracken when the wind in this night only half-grown-dark is entangled in it.

The gradations of colour and shade remain; if you hold your arm out straight, the shadow of your finger becomes sharp as if outlined in pencil. But the light that filters in through the latticework of leaves above my head will no longer spill in puddles on the ground, it will scatter crescents of sunlight, stamped out like coins of tin. For a few minutes strips of shadow, as wide as a hand, will move across the land one after the other, waves of bright black, as fast as the eye can follow. These are the shadows cast by a gust of wind; the same wind that causes the stars to shine in the night; that is Eriugena's darkness that gives rise to all things: *omne quod manifestatur, lumen est.*

Praxedes; she
did not walk, but
hovered and
remained motion-
less for hours
staring at the light
that she saw drip-
ping from heaven
like molten iron.
Depicted with her
sister Prudentiana,
whose blood
she caught in a
bowl as she was
martyred.

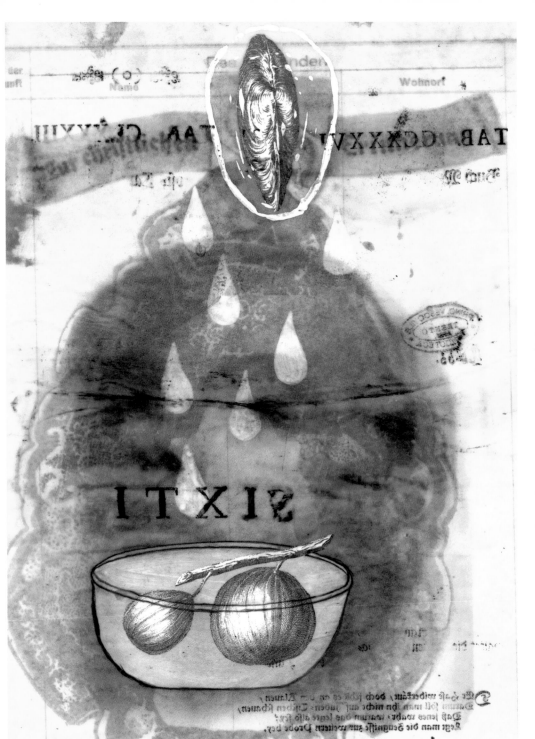

XX

The total eclipse of the sun will only be observable 50 miles out in the Atlantic, but just the same I've made myself a little *camera lucida* out of cardboard, so I can witness this world theatre that you angels are performing. From the land at least a glimpse of your great stage projection must still be visible, I reckon. But you angels probably call it a theophany, the appearance of the invisible, the ineffable light, about which cannot be said *what*, only *that* it is.

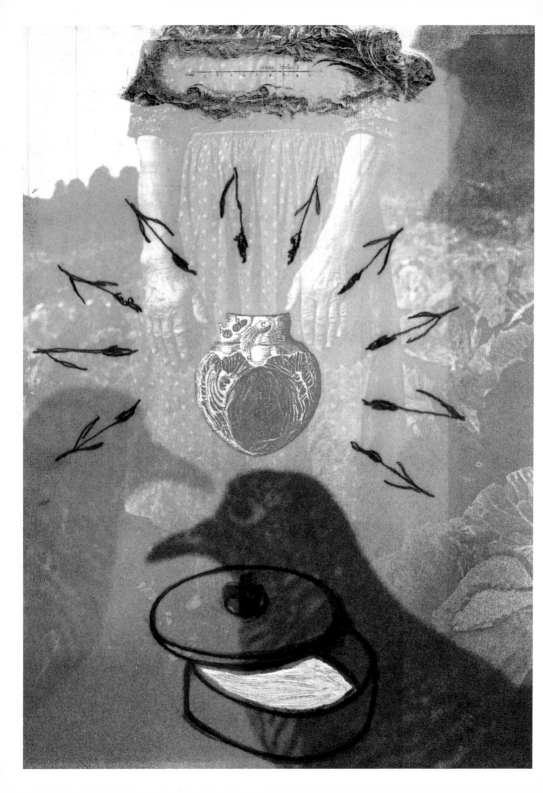

As it is when in the union with fire the iron is freed from inside the ore, Eriugena claims, so it is with human nature made manifest in the light of God: the iron retains the fire within it.

Its palls of smoke now extend at least from the clouds to the line of the horizon, but the wind a solar eclipse brings with it will penetrate the clouds for a moment to allow a glimpse into that most profound darkness, that great maw in which the moon almost completely vanishes. The only white that remains is something like the tip of a dark tongue. And then this half-ring will be interwoven, broken through in places, with scarlet and crimson gaps of a light that falls across the pitted face of the moon, its valleys, craters and mountain ranges breaking the line of the edge: Baily's pearls. It is a flickering, half-wreath, a pale reflection of the corona, glowing incandescent like liquid ore in a forge, molten metal that flows across the skillet of the sun.

The sky cools and solidifies. The moon slowly detaches itself and the sun moves into the next bank of cloud, deeper into the slag of its darkness: Eriugena's *lux inacessibilis*. It was in this darkness that he first became aware of his God, face to face and yet blind; and the Seraphim had closed their wings over their heads and feet

Hilda, Abbess of Streaneshalch, an abbey in the North of England, that pursued ancient Celtic customs; during a solar eclipse, she prevented wild birds from ravaging the cornfields but was blinded as she did it.

135

to ward off the dark light. The information sheets distributed by the planetarium have given warnings about looking directly into the sun, however tempting it might seem. The retina is burnt without you being aware and the damage cannot be reversed: *per quem ad principalem lumen, patrem accessum habemus.*

Regardless whether illusion or belief, it is above all spectacle. And creation a divine comedy, followed by a posse of buffoons who gape with their eyes wide, blind and blinded. The whole motley clientele gathers at Hackett's Pub. And none of them have seen anything in this rain; it didn't even get really dark, just a bit grey, like a thunder cloud; if one didn't know it was happening one wouldn't have noticed anything at all. Bretons are there; Ant, a still and resolutely smiling Turk stands behind the bar; the Italian painter who has built himself a cave on a patch of land is quoting Plato's allegory the wrong way round; the tourists won't let themselves be robbed of their Celtic twilight and the half-dozen others who have pitched up here and who don't want to be tourists and won't ever be locals are claiming householders' rights for their Irish paradise. A mob of faces I know by sight without remembering the individual names. And of course I'm also there at the bar, a phoney saint to all appearances, and that girl with the narrow shoulders and her hair up in a bun walks past me without saying hello.

The toothless local with sideburns right down his cheeks has been annoying me for a while; he's been grumbling incessantly and elbowing me in the ribs. Damn it, I interrupt him, speak up. That's my beer you've been drinking the whole time, he replies. I only have a five-pound note on me, but no one will change it for me because they were withdrawn from circulation ages ago, along with their portrait of Scottus Eriugena: morose in his buttoned-up fur, bald head like an eternal acolyte, though his features must have been done from imagination. Through the open door one can see the rain pelting down, it's raining cats and dogs, the company of gods invisible in the clouds.

A pack of fools searching for God knows what and finding God knows what, the painter bawls after the third pint; silhouettes on a wall; everything pressing from light into darkness. For me it's still a bit early for the meaning of life, but he won't give up, wants to know what I believe in. Not one thing or another. Why I write? Because of you, the girl with the red hair and the eyes that don't know where to look; but that is nobody's business. So I answer that I believe in nothing, but because that is hard, I make a pretext of the light and the spectacle. In doing that I've said nothing, and nor have I betrayed you.

Bishop's Luck, Cappaghglass
May 1999–August 2000

Ingeborg, the Danish Princess famed for her shining red hair, was left by her husband for another woman and took up with a wandering player.

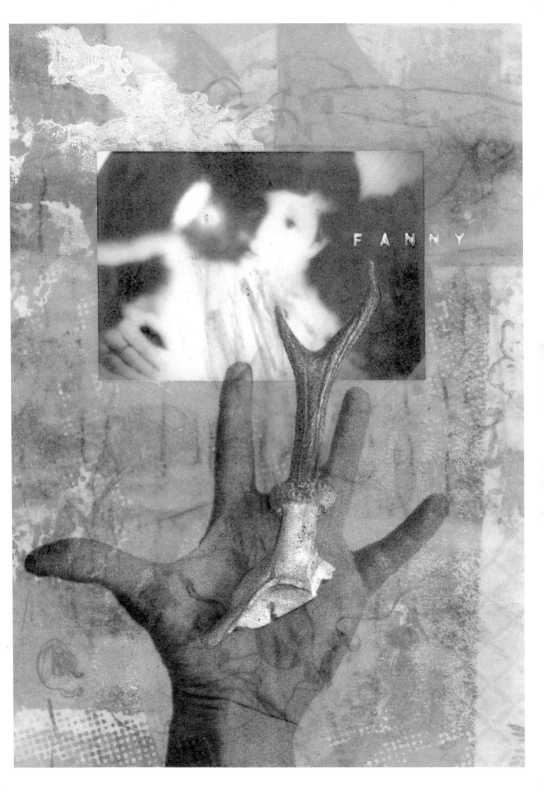

Ivan, the son of a
Dalmatian Prince,
rejected the crown
and lived in many
caves as a hermit,
praying for release
from the demons
that plagued him.

*Original size
of the images
20 x 28.5 cm*

*Drawing, photo-
graph, silkscreen
and linoleum
stamp on paper*